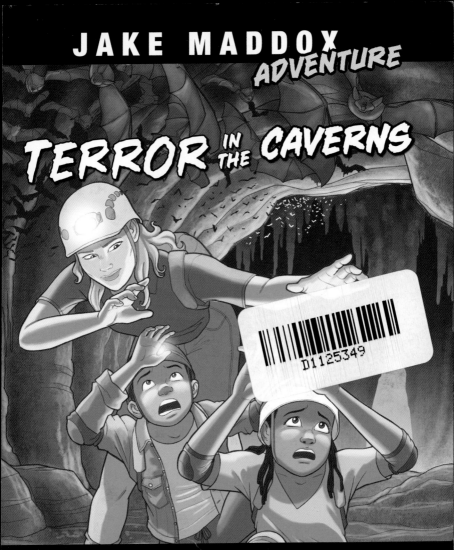

JAKE MADDOX
ADVENTURE

TERROR IN THE CAVERNS

BY JAKE MADDOX

Text by Shawn Pryor
Illustrated by Giuliano Aloisi

STONE ARCH BOOKS
a capstone imprint

Jake Maddox Adventure is published by Stone Arch Books,
an imprint of Capstone.
1710 Roe Crest Drive
North Mankato, Minnesota 56003
www.capstonepub.com

Library of Congress Cataloging-in-Publication Data
Names: Maddox, Jake, author. | Pryor, Shawn, coauthor. | Aloisi,
Giuliano, illustrator.
Title: Terror in the caverns / [Jake Maddox] ; text by Shawn Pryor ;
    illustrated by Giuliano Aloisi.
Description: North Mankato, Minnesota : Stone Arch Books, [2021] |
Series: Jake Maddox adventure | Audience: Ages 8-12. | Audience:
Grades 4-6. |
    Summary: Mia and Deshawn are not excited by a surprise stop at
Maximum Caverns during a family vacation, but when their guide,
Raven, is injured, the siblings must navigate an advanced route
and summon help. Includes glossary, discussion questions, writing
prompts, and information about spelunking.
Identifiers: LCCN 2020034828 (print) | LCCN 2020034829 (ebook) |
ISBN 9781515882275 (hardcover) | ISBN 9781515883364 (paperback)
ISBN 9781515892359 (ebook pdf)
Subjects: CYAC: Caving--Fiction. | Caves--Fiction. | Brothers and
    sisters--Fiction. | Fear--Fiction. | Wounds and injuries--Fiction.
Classification: LCC PZ7.M25643 Teh 2021 (print) | LCC PZ7.M25643
(ebook) | DDC [Fic]--dc23
LC record available at https://lccn.loc.gov/2020034828
LC ebook record available at https://lccn.loc.gov/2020034829"

Designer: Sarah Bennett

TABLE OF CONTENTS

CHAPTER 1

SURPRISE!

Mia and Deshawn sat in the backseat of their parents' SUV as they traveled down the highway. Deshawn fiddled through apps on his smartphone. He was trying his best to be as patient as possible. But it was difficult! Mia, Deshawn's older sister, was reading a book.

"My maps app is telling me that we're only one hundred and seventy-five miles away from Action World! Only a few more hours until we arrive at the greatest amusement park of all time!" Deshawn said, looking over at his sister. "How can you read a book at a time like this? Aren't you excited?"

Mia placed a bookmark in her book and closed it. "Reading makes the trip go by faster. And quit wasting your data. Mom and Dad already have their GPS running; they don't need a backup map reader," Mia said.

Deshawn turned off the app. "I know. I'm just excited to get there. I've waited all summer for this! I have a list of rides I want us to go on. Don't forget you promised you would ride the Beastacular Coaster of Fear with me."

Mia smiled and said, "Of course! And you have to be my copilot on the MegaSpace Rocket ride."

"You know it!" said Deshawn.

Their dad turned around to face Mia and Deshawn, interrupting their conversation. "Mom and I are glad that you're excited about our family vacation," he said. "But we have another surprise for you."

"What surprise?" asked Mia and Deshawn in unison.

"In a moment, your mom will be able to show you," said Dad. "Take the next exit, sweetheart."

"Next exit?" Deshawn asked. "But that will take us off the highway and away from Action World."

"Don't worry," said Mom. "This stop will only take us a few hours." She swiftly left the highway and the most direct route to Action World.

"Plus," their dad continued, "we're going to be at Action World for over a week, so we're not going to miss anything. The two of you will like this surprise. You'll see."

"But—" said Deshawn.

"No buts, young man," Dad said sternly. "Just be patient and enjoy this stop along the way."

Deshawn put his head down in annoyance as the family's SUV exited the highway. This was not the first time their dad had thrown a surprise at the family.

I just want to get to Action World. This stop we're taking better be good, he thought.

Mia picked up her book and continued reading. She seemed unbothered.

"There's no need to pout, little bro," Mia said. "We'll get there soon enough."

After a few minutes, their mom pulled into a parking lot. After Deshawn got out, he saw a big sign next to a visitor's center.

"Maximum Caverns?" he asked, reading the sign. "This is our surprise? We're looking at caves?"

"We know how much the two of you liked the movie *Daytona Jones and the Cavern of Magic,* so we figured that you would like a tour through an actual cave!" Mom said.

"I don't want to do this," said Deshawn.

Mia shrugged her shoulders. "Seems OK to me, I guess."

"Everybody out of the vehicle," said Dad. "Adventure awaits the two of you!"

CHAPTER 2

SPELUNKING OR BUST

At Maximum Caverns, a tour guide named Raven talked to Mia and Deshawn as their parents looked on.

"Since this is your first time cave spelunking—" Raven began.

"Spell-what-did-you-say?" asked Deshawn.

Raven laughed and explained, "Spelunking is the exploration of caverns. Maximum Caverns is the fourth-largest cave system in the entire world. We have multiple cavern trails including belowground caverns, underground lakes, backcountry campsites, campgrounds, and more."

Raven took a breath and continued, "You two will be going on our underground walking tour, so we'll need to make sure you have some basic supplies."

Mia seemed a tad unsure. She had never been in a cave before. "What will we need for going underground?" she asked.

"Well, you both have on pants, which is good, because even though it's a warm summer day outside, it's going to be a lot cooler once we enter the cave." Raven handed Mia and Deshawn a backpack each.

"These backpacks are heavy," said Mia.

"They hold all the proper items for a trip through the cave. You'll need knee and elbow pads, a flashlight, a headlamp, an electric lamp, water, some snacks, a map, a first-aid kit, and some fluorescent flagging tape. In case we get lost, these items will come in handy," said Raven.

"We don't have time to get lost!" Deshawn said. "There's an amusement park we need to get to!" He dropped the pack and stormed off.

"Deshawn! Get back here and apologize to Raven," their mom yelled.

Mia looked at Raven and her parents. "I'm sorry about this, Raven. I'll go talk to him."

After a few minutes, Mia caught up with Deshawn, who was sitting on a park bench, clearly still upset.

"Deshawn, what are you doing? Did you really need to make a scene?" asked Mia.

"I don't want to be here. I want to be at Action World," said Deshawn.

Mia sat next to Deshawn and put her hand on his shoulder. "Look," she said, "I really don't want to do this tour either, but it's only going to take an hour to do the easy route. So let's just do this and be done with it. Then we can get back on the road, OK?"

Deshawn thought about what Mia said. *I guess this won't take that long,* he told himself. He took a deep breath.

"Fine," said Deshawn. "Let's get this over with." When Deshawn and Mia started walking back toward their tour guide and parents, he asked, "How mad did I make Mom and Dad?"

Mia grimaced. "Let's just say that you should apologize to everyone immediately, or the only place we'll being going after this cave tour is home."

CHAPTER 3

THE TOUR BEGINS!

Raven led Mia and Deshawn into the cave to start on what Raven called the E-Z Walking Tour. They had their gear and backpacks on tightly. Their parents waved and took a seat on a park bench not too far away.

Within a few minutes of Mia, Deshawn, and Raven being in the cave, the temperature dropped.

"Wow, it sure got cold fast," Mia said. She noticed how tight the space had become inside the cavern. She kept looking back at the entrance, which got smaller and smaller the farther they walked.

"The caves here keep the cold air in place. The cold air flow makes it harder for warmer surface air to enter the cave. Although, not all caves are cold," said Raven. "Depending on where the cave is located around the world, it could have drastic temperature changes."

"So what's the difference between a cave and a cavern?" Deshawn asked.

"A cave is any cavity in the ground that's so large some parts don't get direct sunlight. A cavern is a natural area in the ground within the rocks below. A cavern can be called a cave, but not all caves are caverns, if that makes sense," Raven replied.

"It kind of makes sense," he said.

The path they followed took a steep decline.

As the group went down, Mia lost sight of the entrance. She became nervous. The rock walls felt like they were closing in on her.

"Umm . . . how deep will this tour take us? And is the whole tour through the cave so . . . small?" she asked.

"The tour's about two miles. We won't go too deep," replied Raven. "And don't worry—there are some spots where the caverns open up a bit."

Mia exhaled. "That's a relief."

Deshawn fiddled with his flashlight. "I don't think my flashlight is bright enough. Is the light on my headgear bright? It's so dark in here," Deshawn said. "Mia, are my lights bright enough?"

Mia patted his back. "Your lights are fine, little brother."

The trail led the group around a bend and into a new cave. Raven pointed up as they all looked up at the massive ceiling.

"Wow," said Deshawn, "Daytona Jones swung on those things in the movie!"

"Those things," Raven began, "are called stalactites. These stalactites were formed by minerals and water from the cave ceiling as they slowly trickled downward to form a hanging structure from the ceiling."

"I wouldn't want one of those to fall on me," said Deshawn.

"Don't worry, Deshawn. These stalactites aren't going anywhere anytime soon," said Raven.

"That's good to know!" Mia said. The group continued to wind their way through the cavern. After making a turn, Raven put her arm out, signaling them all to stop.

Raven whispered, "If you look up and to your left, you'll see a family of little brown bats. Keep your voice down—"

Mia cut her off. "Keep those things away from me!" she whispered and gave Raven a disapproving look.

Deshawn pulled out his phone, preparing to take a picture. "My friends at home will never believe this!" he whispered.

Raven reached for Deshawn's smartphone. "No, don't take any pictures with flash—"

But it was too late. Deshawn took rapid-fire pictures.

Flash-flash-flash-flash!

Reacting to the light of the flashes, the family of bats woke up and headed right toward the small tour group.

Mia dropped. She waved her hands above her head furiously, hoping to keep the bats out of her hair. "Get them away from me!" she screamed.

"Don't let them get me, Mia! Don't let them get me!" said Deshawn.

"Stay calm and get low, kids! They won't hurt you!" yelled Raven as she tried to bring Mia and Deshawn closer to her.

The two kids struggled against Raven in their panic. As Mia ducked one way and Deshawn the other, the trio all tripped, falling off the raised path. They tumbled down a dark, dangerous slope on the side, leading them off the trail.

CHAPTER 4

OFF THE TRAIL

Groggy from the fall, Mia and Deshawn got up slowly from the ground. The area of the cave that they were in now was much colder than where they were before, and much darker. There was a faint dripping noise that could be heard in the distance.

"That was an awful fall. Felt like it took forever," said Mia. "Are you OK, Deshawn?"

"I think I am. Raven broke most of my fall—oh no, Raven!" he said.

The two went over to her and gently nudged her awake. Raven grabbed her right leg. The two could tell she was in pain.

"I think my leg is broken. This hurts something awful," Raven said.

"Are you going to be all right?" Mia asked.

"I'm not going to be able to walk us out of here," Raven said. "Mia, can you get my walkie-talkie from my backpack, please? I can't reach it."

"Sure thing," Mia said, getting the walkie-talkie and handing it to Raven. "Will it work down here?"

"Yes, the signal on these is very strong, so I'll be able to call HQ and get us help in no time," Raven said, trying to turn it on. She fiddled with it for a few moments. "Well, I stand corrected. My walkie-talkie must've broken when we fell."

"I left my phone in the car, so I can't call for help, either," Mia said.

She paced back and forth for a bit and then angrily turned toward her brother.

"This is all your fault, Deshawn!" Mia yelled at him. "You just *had* to take pictures of those stupid bats. Now Raven is really hurt, and we can't get out of here!"

"I never wanted to be here in the first place, remember? You were the one who insisted that we do this tour," Deshawn said. "But whatever, I'll call our parents and let them know we need help."

Deshawn reached for his phone and looked at the screen. "Oh no, my phone must've gotten busted up when we fell! The screen's cracked, and it won't turn on."

"What are we going to do? Raven needs help!" Mia said.

Raven interrupted them. "Hey, the first thing both of you need to do is calm down. Come over here and sit."

Mia and Deshawn went and sat next to Raven.

"We'll find a way out of this," said Raven. "Pull out the first-aid kits and let me check both of you for any possible cuts or injuries."

Mia helped Raven take off her backpack and handed it to her. Both kids sat with Raven in a small circle as she turned on her electric lamp. The lamp's light bounced off the rough cavern walls as Raven, Mia, and Deshawn got to work.

CHAPTER 5

A SCARY QUEST

After Mia and Deshawn helped bandage and stabilize Raven's leg, they checked each other for scrapes and bumps. After they had finished, Raven still could not put any pressure on her leg.

"How are we going to get help for Raven? How do we even get out of here? None of us can climb back up there," said Deshawn, looking up. "That is way too steep for us."

Mia scratched her head. "And it doesn't help that we don't have any way to call for help. We can't just leave Raven here; we don't even know where we are."

Raven looked over her surroundings and noticed something on one of the walls. "Mia, can you shine your flashlight up and over to the left?" she asked.

Mia slowly scanned the cave wall with her flashlight.

When Raven saw what she was looking for, she said, "Aha! Do you see the large strips of reflective tape up there?"

"Yes, I see them!" Mia replied. "It looks like a shiny number fifteen on the wall."

"What does that mean?" Deshawn asked.

"All of our trails have number markers so tour guides and tourists can understand and navigate through the caverns," said Raven as she pulled her map from her backpack. "And according to the map, marker fifteen means that . . . uh-oh."

"'Uh-oh'? What do you mean 'uh-oh'? What's wrong?" asked Mia.

Raven let out a large sigh. "We're now on the advanced cavern trail."

Deshawn's concerns grew. "'Advanced'? What does that mean?"

"It means that the path to get us out of here is a little more difficult without adult supervision for both of you," said Raven. "Instead of a one- or two-mile trail, it's six miles long. We're closer to the exit than the entrance, but the last part of the trail is very tough, and could be very difficult for both of you."

"OK, so we just wait for the next advanced trail group to come through and help us," said Deshawn. "Another group should be coming around anytime now, right?"

Raven checked her watch and then shook her head. "The last advanced group tour ended an hour ago, and the next one isn't until tomorrow morning."

"We can't be trapped down here all night. What if there are bears down here? We have to get out!" Deshawn said.

"There are no bears in these caves, Deshawn," said Mia. "But you're right—we can't wait all night for someone to rescue us. Raven needs medical help."

Deshawn put his hands up in frustration. "So, what are we going to do?"

"We're going to take the advanced trail and get help for Raven," Mia said. "It's the only choice we have."

CHAPTER 6

A TIGHT SQUEEZE

Mia and Deshawn packed their backpacks and put on their headlamps. Raven helped them attach carabiners onto their belts and connected them to each other with a piece of rope. The rope ensured they would stay close in case of emergency.

With encouraging words from Raven, the two began the journey through the advanced trail—alone. The path they were on was dark and narrow. Mia checked her map constantly, while Deshawn placed reflective tape on the walls and ground as markers in case they became lost.

"I hope that Raven will be all right," said Deshawn.

"Raven is going to be OK," said Mia. "She has a blanket that will keep her warm. Plus, her lamp has enough power for the next twelve hours, and she has some snacks and water. Once we make it out of here, we'll get her help immediately."

Deshawn gripped the rope tightly as they walked through a narrow section of the cavern. "What if *we* don't make it?" he asked quietly.

"Don't say that!" Mia took in a sharp breath. "We're going to make it out. Put some reflective tape on the wall, OK?"

"OK," said Deshawn as he marked the wall with the tape. "There, all done. Let me know when I need to put another one up, OK?" Deshawn noticed Mia wasn't saying anything. "OK?" he repeated. "Hey, what's wrong, Mia?"

Mia couldn't respond. Her breaths moved in and out quickly.

And as they continued to walk, Mia tried to keep calm as the cavern became more and more narrow. To Mia, it felt as if the walls had come to life and were trying to squeeze her.

"Mia, what's wrong?" asked Deshawn again.

"The map says we're going to have to crawl through the tunnel for the next three hundred and fifty feet to get to the other side of the trail," said Mia quickly before taking a deep breath. "I . . . I'm claustrophobic. I'm really scared of small spaces."

"Why didn't you tell Mom and Dad before they made us go on this tour?" said Deshawn.

"Because I didn't want to let them down, and I didn't want anyone to know," said Mia. "And since we were doing the E-Z Walking Tour, I figured I could handle it."

Mia looked around frantically. "But look where we are now," she added.

Deshawn took Mia's hand. He'd never seen his sister like this, and he was worried.

"Hey, take a deep breath and slowly let it out," he said. "You keep breathing fast like that, and you're going to hyperinflate."

Mia tried to laugh. "You mean *hyperventilate*."

"That's what I said, I think," said Deshawn. An idea suddenly came to him. "Remember in the Daytona Jones movie when his sidekick was stuck in a tight space and started to panic?"

"Yes," Mia said. "What about it?"

"To calm him down Daytona Jones told him to think about open spaces. After awhile his breathing returned to normal. Can you do that?" he asked.

Mia smiled at her brother. "I can try."

Mia started thinking about her favorite places: a neighborhood park, a big, grassy field behind her school, and her backyard at home.

After a few moments, Mia started to calm down.

"I'm going to be OK," she said. "Besides, I have to keep going, whether I like it or not." She took another deep breath. "Let's get ready to crawl. I'll go first, and you follow behind me. If you need to take a break or need me to slow down, just tug on the rope, OK?"

Deshawn nodded. "Let's do this," he said.

Mia and Deshawn started crawling. Mia could feel gusts of air as they continued to crawl on the bumpy surface of the tunnel.

"Why would any grown-up want to do this?" said Mia, continuing to crawl.

"Daytona Jones would enjoy something like this," said Deshawn.

"That's because he would get paid for it," Mia joked.

Mia crawled on and on for what felt like a lifetime. Deshawn tugged the rope in order to take a break, and then Mia would start again. Finally, there was a glimmer of light ahead.

"We're almost there!" said Mia. "I wonder what's on the other side?"

"Hopefully not any bats!" said Deshawn.

CHAPTER 7

TROGLOBITES AND TREMORS

Mia climbed out of the tunnel and helped Deshawn out. Brushing off the dirt and debris from the crawl, they were both amazed by the sight before them. A bridge swept over a glittering, underground lake.

As they walked over the bridge, the kids were in awe at how clear the water looked. Way up high, there were a few strands of light coming from the ceiling of the cave. The light made the water glitter, and there was just enough of it to make them both feel comfortable. Halfway across the bridge, Mia saw a small sign.

"It says here that this area is called Troglobite Bay. If you look closely enough, you can see all types of cavern bugs," Mia said.

Deshawn pointed off to the side of the cave wall. "I see one," he said with excitement. "Over there, by the edge. It looks like a see-through snail!"

"And I see a spider that's bigger than my hand!" Mia replied. She continued to read the sign. "Troglobites are small creatures that permanently live underground. Troglobites survive by eating small debris and bat guano. Yuck."

"What's guano?" asked Deshawn.

"You don't want to know," said Mia. "Let's drink some water and get going. We're not out of the dark just yet."

After taking their drinks, they continued their journey. At the end of the bridge, the two faced the next part of the trail.

There were two caverns in front of them. A large cavern was on their left and a smaller, roped-off cavern on the right. The cavern on the right was higher than the one on the left.

Deshawn pointed to a small sign above the left cavern. On it was a symbol of a water droplet. "What do you think that means?" he asked.

"It's on the map too," Mia said. "And according to the map, we'll need to travel through the lower, sloped caverns on the left. It looks like there's a good amount of rough terrain, so we'll have to be slow and careful so we don't hurt ourselves."

"What about the cave on the right?" asked Deshawn.

"That cave is off-limits to everyone," said Mia, tapping her map. "So that way is a no-go."

"I'll mark the bridge, just in case," he said.

After he placed the X on the bridge, they both turned on their flashlights and entered the cave on the left.

In the cave, there were puddles everywhere. Everything seemed damp. Then, they heard an echoing rumble. To Mia, the sound reminded her of a waterfall.

"What was that?" said Mia as they took some steps forward.

"It kind of sounds like water running in a shower, but a lot louder," said Deshawn.

"It sounds like it's coming closer," Mia said. She had to raise her voice so Deshawn could hear her. "And it sounds like a lot of water!" she added.

Deshawn panicked. "What should we do?"

Mia grabbed Deshawn's hand and turned them around to run out of the cave they had just entered.

"Where are we going?" Deshawn asked.

"If there's a flood, it'll fill the lower cave, and I don't feel like swimming," Mia yelled as she took them into the off-limits cavern.

"But why are we in the other cave? We can take the bridge back," Deshawn said.

But as soon as Deshawn took a step toward the bridge, he and Mia saw a massive rush of water exit from the cavern they had just left. The waves crashed into the lake. After everything had settled, there was now so much water that it completely covered the bridge.

The new lake ended only a couple of feet lower than their current cavern's entrance.

"That's why we didn't go back on the bridge," Mia said as the water continued to flow. She opened her map. "Look," she said, motioning Deshawn over. "The map shows that this cave has multiple slopes. There's no connection to any water sources on this side, but it doesn't show where this cave ends."

"Good thinking, Mia," Deshawn said. "We could've been washed out by the flood." He then looked at Mia. "But where did all that water come from?" They studied the map for clues.

"It looks like if things were normal, we would've kept on going the way we were supposed to," Mia said. "From there, we would've hit another fork in the cave, and gone to the right. There's a big water drop symbol on that part."

"That's the same symbol that was above the other cave!" Deshawn said.

Mia looked at the water drop symbol on the map, then looked at the map key.

"The big water drop means that's an area that can possibly flood," Mia said. "It also says if the air temperature increases within that area, water overflow near that section of the cave can cause floods."

"Well, there must've been a big heat wave somewhere, because that was a lot of water! At least we're safe for now," Deshawn said.

Mia nodded. "We're going to be OK. We'll have to take this off-limits cave trail and see where it leads us. Hopefully, it gets us out of here."

CHAPTER 8

THE MINING SHAFT

Mia and Deshawn walked on. Their new route was dark and cold. Deshawn felt uneasy and constantly fiddled with his flashlight.

"It's like the cave is absorbing my light," said Deshawn. "It's pure darkness in here!"

"I know," Mia replied. "We're going to have to be very careful."

Deshawn's flashlight stopped working suddenly. He began to panic. *I'm never going to see the light of day again*, he thought.

"It's too dark in here," Deshawn said. "Something's going to get us." He backed up and hit a wall.

"It's OK. I'm right here," Mia said. "I'm not going to let anything happen to you."

"It's just that," Deshawn began. "The real reason I didn't want to go on the cave tour is because I'm afraid of the dark."

"Why didn't you say anything?" Mia asked.

"I thought you would make fun of me," he admitted.

"You should've at least told Mom and Dad. They would've canceled the tour," she said.

"No, they would've thought I was making excuses so we could get back on the road to Action World," said Deshawn.

Mia paused for a moment. "OK, maybe you're right. Give me your flashlight," said Mia. She looked it over as they walked on. "Let me see if I can fix—"

Mia's words were cut short as she tripped and fell.

"I'm fine. I just tripped over this thick wire," said Mia as she stood up.

But the wire was, in fact, a bar. And that bar connected to a power switch. Mia flipped the switch, which turned on a trail of lights in the cave.

"Wow! This looks like the abandoned mining cave from the Daytona Jones movie!" said Deshawn.

Mia smiled. "It does, doesn't it? Well, now we have a bright path and a trail of what looks to be mine tracks to lead us somewhere," she said.

As they walked through the abandoned mine, they noticed rusty pickaxes, old mining hats, and other types of tools. All were aged by time and nature.

"This is amazing! Look, there's even a mining cart!" said Deshawn. He raced toward it, dragging Mia along.

"Hold on! We're still linked together with rope," said Mia, but Deshawn ignored her. "Slow down!"

"Sorry, I got excited," said Deshawn as he hopped into the cart.

"What are you doing? Get out of that cart before something happens!" yelled Mia.

Deshawn brushed off any concern. "Pfft, this thing is so old. There's no way it's going to move," he said.

The cart started to move—slowly at first. But then, it went a little faster and faster and faster. Soon Mia had to run so she wouldn't get dragged by the cart.

"Pull the brake! Pull the brake!" Mia yelled.

Deshawn panicked and said, "I don't know if it has a brake!"

Mia finally caught up with the cart. She hopped in and grabbed on to Deshawn.

"Come on," she said. "We've got to jump out of here before it's—"

"Too late!" Deshawn said, finishing her sentence. The mining cart quickly raced the tracks with blinding speed!

"Hang on!" Mia yelled.

CHAPTER 9

CARTS AND CLIMBING

The mining cart raced through the cavern tracks, sending sparks left and right with every turn. Deshawn looked ahead and saw a very sharp turn ahead.

"We're going too fast to take the turn ahead. We'll crash," he said.

The turn would be coming at any moment, and they needed to slow down. Mia spotted a lever on the side of the cart. She hoped it was the brake.

Mia pulled on the lever as hard as she could. The brakes activated, sending sparks everywhere.

"Hold on!" she said. To her relief, the cart began to slow down. "I think we're going to make it."

They approached the turn at a slower speed, staying on the tracks.

Deshawn let out a sigh. "Phew, that was close," he said.

"At least we can control the speed of the cart now," said Mia. "And hopefully find a way out of here."

They rode the cart with ease through the cavern. Mia controlled the brakes while Deshawn worked as a lookout. Deshawn was having a ton of fun riding the cart. Too soon for his liking, they were stopped by a small wall of sandbags. They were at the end of their ride. Mia quickly exited the cart, but Deshawn stayed.

"That was awesome," he said. "Let's do it again!"

"Absolutely not," said Mia. "You may have had fun, but while we've been in this cave, your actions have had some serious consequences! Raven is hurt because you took pictures without thinking, and what if the brake on the cart hadn't worked? It could've been the end of us."

Deshawn paused for a moment. He looked down and then met his sister's eyes. "I never really looked at it that way," he said. "I should think before I act. If I would've done that, then maybe we wouldn't be in this mess. I'm sorry, Mia."

Mia gave Deshawn a hug. "I forgive you. But let's make good choices from here on out, OK?"

"All right. I promise I will," Deshawn said, and he meant it.

"Look, over there," Mia said and pointed at an exit sign farther down the path. "There's our way out! We're almost out of here!"

Once they reached the sign, Deshawn looked up. It was a long way to the top. He became nervous. "But in order for us to get to that door, we have to climb up that very, very tall ladder," he said.

The steel fixed ladder was at least fifty feet in height and surrounded by flared caging. Full of cobwebs and specks of rust, it had clearly not been used in a very long time. *This is not meant for children*, Mia thought.

Mia took Deshawn's backpack and made sure that the rope connecting them both together was strong and secure.

"OK, I want you to go first," she said. "I'll follow you from behind. I know it's scary, but we have to do this, and I won't let you fall."

Deshawn took a deep breath, exhaled, and started climbing the ladder slowly. He concentrated on one rung at a time. Mia followed him.

"We're about a quarter of the way up, little brother," said Mia. "You're doing great!"

As they continued to climb, both felt how tired they were. The events of their adventure had taken a toll. But they knew they couldn't stop. Each step brought them closer to making it out and getting help for Raven.

"Halfway there!" said Mia.

After a few more minutes, Mia and Deshawn were at the top of the platform.

"We did it, sis! We made it!" said Deshawn, hugging his sister.

"We did it," Mia repeated, opening the door. They were blinded by the sunlight. Once their eyes adjusted, they found themselves in the middle of the park. Mia saw people off in the distance.

"Help!" Mia shouted. "Somebody help!"

A park employee raced over. "What's wrong? Are you OK?" he asked.

Mia answered, "Our tour guide is hurt. We think her leg is broken. She's near marker fifteen on the advanced trail. Hurry, she needs help!"

CHAPTER 10

WHAT AN ADVENTURE!

Mia and Deshawn sat with their parents outside of the main office of Maximum Caverns. The kids were really worried about Raven.

"Both of you were on the advanced trail?" asked their dad.

"And you were almost washed away by a flood?" asked their mom.

Deshawn interrupted. "And we rode in a mine cart!"

"What?!" their parents replied.

"It's a long story," Mia said. "I just hope the paramedics were able to get to Raven."

"Look!" said Deshawn, pointing to the E-Z Walking Tour cave entrance.

The paramedics were wheeling Raven out on a stretcher. Mia, Deshawn, and their parents rushed over to her.

"Is she going to be OK?" asked Mia.

"She'll be fine," said one of the paramedics. "We'll get her in a cast to make sure her leg properly heals."

Raven saw Mia and Deshawn and smiled. "You two really stepped up," she said. "Thank you both. But next time, let's keep our phones in our pockets, OK?"

"Yes, ma'am," said Deshawn.

"Get better soon," said Mia.

"I will," said Raven. "And thank you again." The paramedics took Raven to the ambulance.

The sun started to set as the family walked back to their car.

"I don't know about you, but I think we've had enough adventure for today," said Mia.

"Me too," said Deshawn.

"Does that mean that you don't want to go to Action World?" Mom asked.

"We've come too far to turn back now," said Mia.

"Let's go!" said Deshawn.

AUTHOR BIO

Shawn Pryor is the creator and co-writer of the all-ages graphic novel mystery series Cash & Carrie, writer of *Kentucky Kaiju*, and writer and co-creator of the 2019 GLYPH-nominated football/drama series Force. He is also the author of the Jake Maddox Sports Stories title *Diamond Double Play*. In his free time, Shawn enjoys reading, cooking, listening to music, and talking about why Zack from the *Mighty Morphin Power Rangers* is the greatest superhero of all time.

ILLUSTRATOR BIO

After graduating from the Institute for Cinema and Television in Rome, Italy, in 1995, Giuliano Aloisi began working as an animator, layout artist, and storyboard artist on several series and games for RAI TV. He went on to illustrate for the comic magazine *Lupo Alberto* and for *Cuore*, a satirical weekly magazine. Giuliano continues to work as an animator and illustrator for advertising companies and educational publishing.

GLOSSARY

abandoned (uh-BAN-duhnd)—empty or left

carabiner (kar-uh-BEE-nuhr)—an oval-shaped metal clip; used to connect and hold ropes

cavern (KA-vuhrn)—a deep, hollow place underground

claustrophobic (klaw-struh-FOH-bik)—having an extreme fear of small or tight spaces

debris (duh-BREE)—the scattered pieces of something that has been broken or destroyed

fluorescent (fluh-RES-uhnt)—a visible light given off by minerals when certain forms of energy, such as ultraviolet light, are applied to them

hyperventilate (HYE-pur-ven-tuh-LATE)—to breathe at a difficult, fast rate

mineral (MIN-ur-uhl)—a material found in nature that is not made by a plant or animal; minerals have crystal structures

paramedic (pa-ruh-MEH-dik)—a person who treats patients before they reach the hospital

spelunking (spuh-LUNG-king)—the exploration of caves

stalactites (stuh-LAK-tites)—growths that hang from the ceiling of a cave and were formed by dripping water

supervision (soo-per-VIZH-uhn)—the act of watching or directing someone as they do something

terrain (tuh-RAYN)—the surface of the land

troglobite (TRAWG-loh-bite)—an animal that can only survive in a cave environment

DISCUSSION QUESTIONS

1. Mia and Deshawn had to travel through the advanced tour in order to escape the caves and get help for Raven. Was there ever a time when you had to do something difficult that you've never done before? Compare your experience with Mia's and Deshawn's.

2. Mia and Deshawn both faced their fears on their cavern tour. Talk about a time when you had to face your fears.

3. In Chapter 9, Mia blames Deshawn for many of the hardships they faced on their tour. Do you think she was right or wrong? Use details from the story to back up your answer.

WRITING PROMPTS

1. In the story, Mia and Deshawn took the advanced trail in order to get help for Raven instead of waiting overnight for help. What would have happened if they had to wait overnight instead? Try rewriting Chapter 5 from a different perspective.

2. In Chapter 1, Deshawn is super excited to get to Action World. Have you ever been on a trip where you were excited to get somewhere? Write about your favorite trip or vacation.

3. At the end of their adventure, Mia and Deshawn have to climb up a ladder to get to the exit. What if the door was locked? Rewrite the ending to explain what the two would do next.

MORE ABOUT CAVE SPELUNKING

- Cave spelunking can be more than just a hobby. Some people who explore caves are interested in conservation or preserving a cavern area for historical reasons. Others might go to gather data about caves. Those people are called speleologists. And there are those who just want to explore caves to learn about the formation of rocks inside it. Those people are called geologists.

- On June 23, 2018, twelve members of a kids soccer team and their coach in Thailand were trapped deep inside a cave that was underneath a mountain. They couldn't leave the way they originally came in. The group was trapped for over two weeks as local citizens, police, the Thai Navy Seals, and rescue teams came together to save them on July 10. The entire effort involved over 10,000 people!

- As of the publication of this book, the world's three longest-known cave systems are:

  - The Mammoth Cave in Kentucky (405 miles/651.7 kilometers)

  - The Sistema Sac Actun/Sistema Dos Ojos in Mexico (198.2 miles/319 km)

  - The Jewel Cave in South Dakota (166.3 miles/267.6 km).

THE FUN DOESN'T STOP HERE!